For Evlynn,
with love, Lauren

For Louie,
love, Polly

Text and stage design copyright © 2006 by Lauren Child
Photographs copyright © 2006 by Polly Borland
First published by Puffin Books in 2006
First U.S. edition, 2006.

For information address Hyperion Books for Children, 114 Fifth Avenue, New York, New York 10011-5690.
This book is set in 13-point Dolly.
1 3 5 7 9 10 8 6 4 2
Printed in China
Reinforced binding
Library of Congress Cataloging-in-Publication Data on file.
ISBN 0-7868-3886-8
Visit www.hyperionbooksforchildren.com

The Princess and the Pea

IN MINIATURE

AFTER THE FAIRY TALE BY
HANS CHRISTIAN ANDERSEN

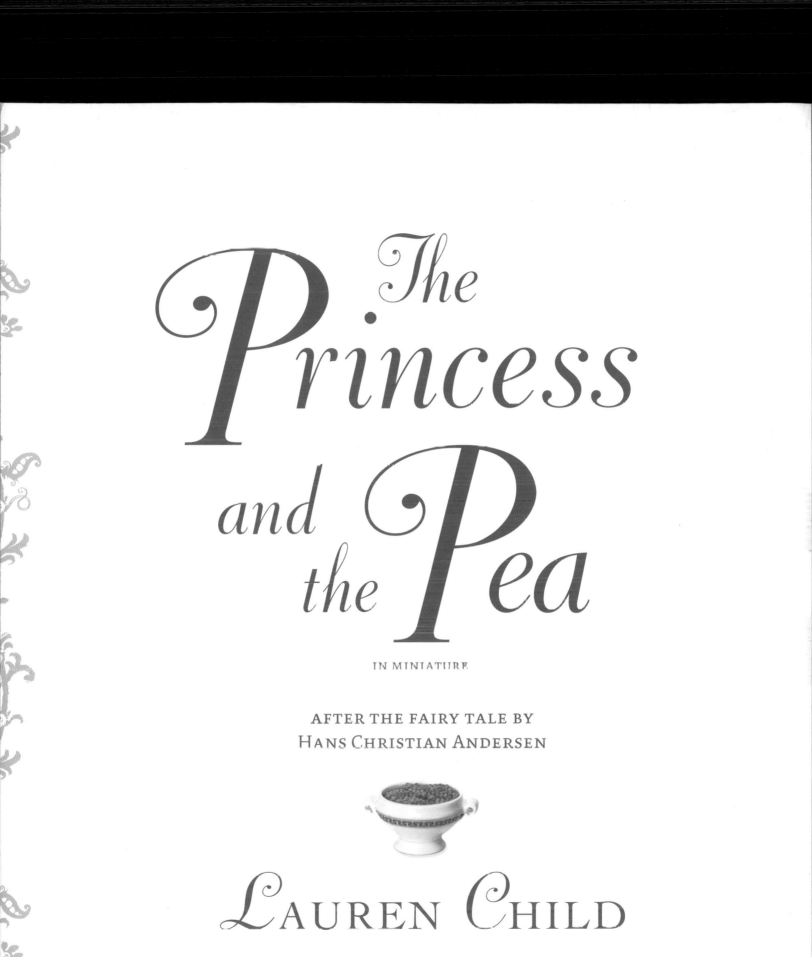

LAUREN CHILD

CAPTURED BY POLLY BORLAND

HYPERION BOOKS FOR CHILDREN
NEW YORK

NCE UPON A
time, many *moons*
ago, *of course*, there
was a king and a
queen who had a
prince for a son.

He was a nice boy and not unpleasant
to look at—in fact, **handsome**—
not *too* **handsome**,
just **handsome**
enough.

⚜

ONE DAY WHEN THE PRINCE was old enough, his parents decided it was time for him to be married. *You know what parents are like, and a prince's parents are no different.*

The prince didn't object to the idea but he did make one condition—

he wanted to marry for *love*.

He was just that kind of romantic *boy*.

He told his father and his mother, "I would gladly marry tomorrow but, whoever she is, she must be **more** *mesmerizing* **than the** *moon* and I must find her **more** *fascinating* **than all the** *stars* **in the sky**. And there must be a *certain… something* about her."

"What *something*?" asked the queen.

"Just… *something*," replied the prince.

"Yes, yes," agreed the king, "that's all very lovely, but our condition is that she must be a **princess** of blue blood and equal in royalness to you."

The prince wasn't all that interested in these details but knew he wouldn't get any peace until he agreed.

So he did.

Now, you may think finding yourself a suitable princess would be easy to do if you are a handsome prince, but you would be wrong—just how many mesmerizing *and* fascinating *princesses do you imagine there are out there?*

Well, the king and queen did all the traditional fairy-tale things in order that their son might be bowled over by the right girl.

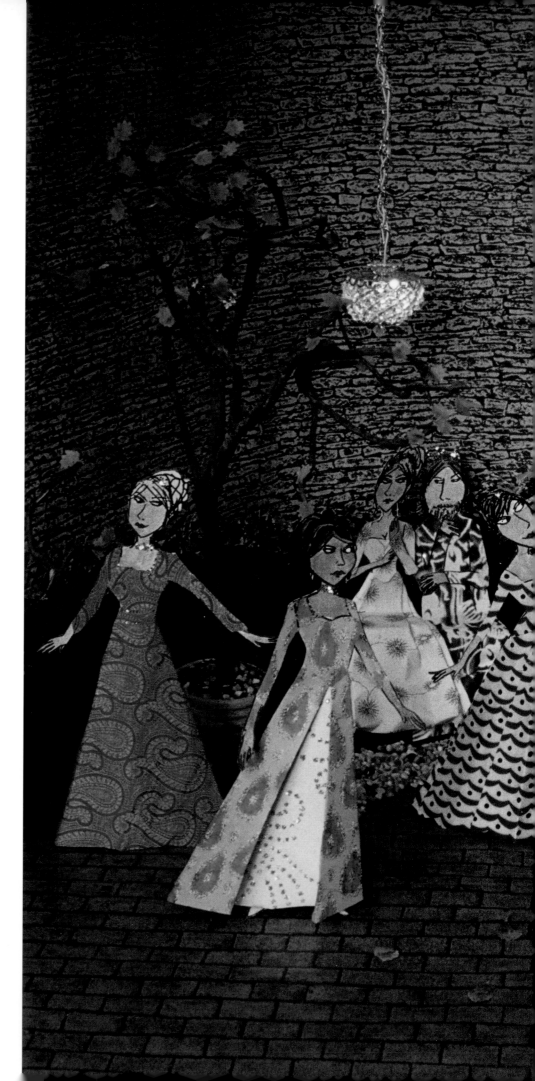

*T*HEY threw a
Royal Ball and invited
all the single royal
girls in the land.

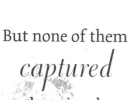

Everyone
said *yes*.

Everyone
danced.

Everyone
had a good time.

But none of them
captured
the prince's
heart.

THE PRINCE EXPLAINED TO THE king and the queen how simply **none** of them was *mesmerizing* or *fascinating*. And **none** of them, **not one** of them, had a *certain... something* about them. No, if he couldn't marry for love, then he would rather live alone for all eternity, gazing at **all the stars in the night sky.** *Not only was he romantic but also a little dramatic.*

The king and the queen said, "The thing is, our dear son, what you are really looking for is a *real* **princess**, and a *real* **princess** is a rare thing indeed."

"They do not grow on trees," said the king.

"No, no, they do not," said the queen.

"You see," said the king, "a *real* **princess** is not only *mesmerizingly* beautiful and *fascinatingly* interesting but, most important of all—"

"She has **manners**," said the queen.

"No one should ever travel without them," said the king.

"No, never, never go anywhere without your **manners**," agreed the queen, taking her elbows off the table.

"The only problem with *real* **princesses**," sighed the king, "is that they are terribly hard to get hold of and they almost never read their mail."

"No indeed," said the queen, "*real* **princesses** are very hard to come by. No one has ever found one by looking, you just have to wait for one to come to you."

UT THE PRINCE, *who rarely listened to his mother's advice,* did the traditional fairy-tale find-yourself-a-bride thing of riding **far** and **wide** looking throughout the kingdom for a *real* princess.

He even rode

far and **wide**

to other people's

kingdoms.

❧

But in **Faärland** all the girls he met were
fascinatingly beautiful but *horribly* vain.

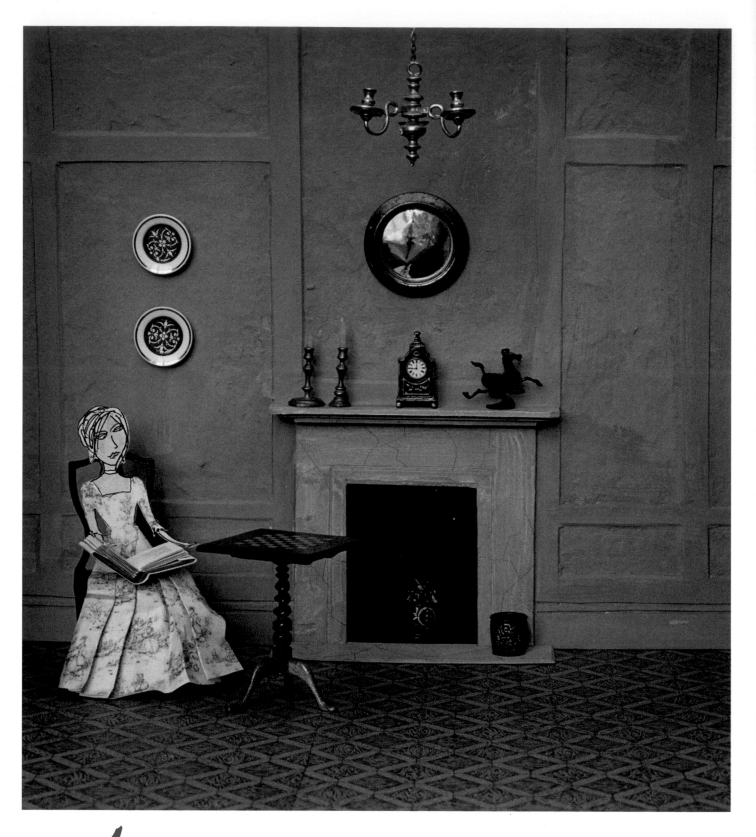

AND in the kingdom of **Schonan** they were all
mesmerizingly clever but *exceedingly* dull.

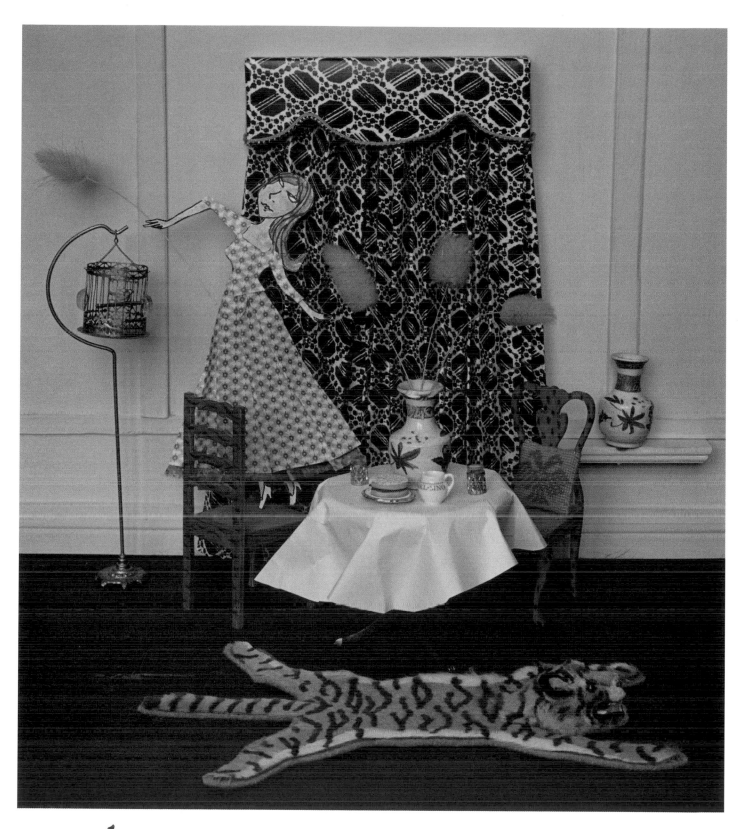

$\mathcal{A}$ND in Harvonia there was a *certain*...
    silliness about them. *I mean, you can see his problem, can't you?*

THE prince came back very downcast. He refused to eat anything for supper, not even the very delicious blackbird pie the royal cook had prepared as a welcome home.

He lit a **candle** in his window and just stood and *gazed* into the night sky.

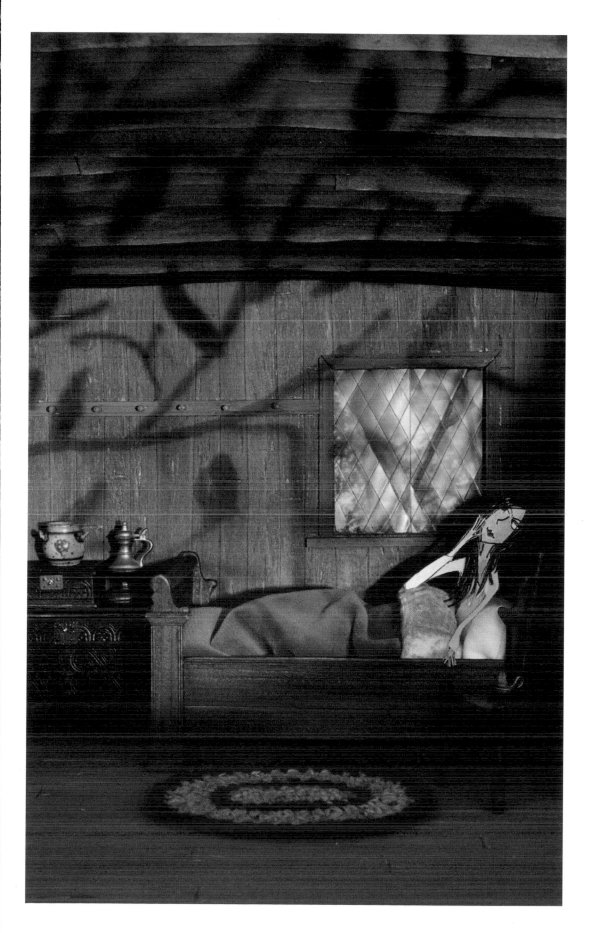

$\mathscr{N}$OT so
far away, in a
treetop house
just over the
mountain, there
was a girl with
the most beautiful
black, black
hair you have ever
seen, *or possibly
never seen.*

❧

She woke up that
night to see the
moon dancing
on her ceiling,
and she popped
on her favorite
pea-green
dress and glided
down the stairs
into the garden.

THE moonlight shone in such a *magical* way that she wondered to herself if it could possibly look as *beautiful* on the other side of the garden wall. So she tripped down the garden path, stepped over a pile of unopened letters, and slipped through the gate, where she saw the *moon* perched on top of the mountain.

"I wonder if the *moon* would be as *beautiful* up there," she thought out loud.

A**ND** it was,
so she continued
walking, right down
the other side of
the mountain until
she came to the
wild woods.

Would it be so
beautiful in
the woods?
considered the girl.

And it was,

it really was.

But just as she came
out of the woods a
dark *cloud* moved
across the *moon*
and **suddenly** …

it wasn't.

BOTHER, THOUGHT THE GIRL.
She could feel a heavy storm brewing. She would
never make it back to her own little tree house in
time. There was nothing for it but to walk on.

So on she walked.

She had not gone more than *seven* steps when
she felt the first heavy drop of rain fall on her cheek.

Bother, thought the girl. Within *three* minutes she was already
soaked to the skin, and her *two* shoes were filling with water.

The *wind* was **howling**,

the *trees* were **creaking** and **cracking** as if they might part

company with their roots, and the *rain* **pounded** down and

the *lightning* **flashed** its forked tongue in the blackened sky.

And the girl began to tire.

It was not umbrella weather, no, an umbrella would have done you no good at all.

"Hmmm, I think I might just catch a *terrible* cold, unless I have the very

good fortune to spot a light in a window . . . but what is the likelihood of that on

this **wild, wild** night in the middle of *nowhere*?" said the girl out loud.

However, as she made her way round the next corner, that's **exactly** what

she saw. Using her very last drop of energy

she climbed the **steep, steep** steps

to the **huge** front door.

*T*HE queen was woken all of a sudden by a very, very loud knock at the palace door. Being a queen, she sensibly woke her husband, an unusually heavy sleeper, and asked him to "go and see who in all the kingdom might be banging on the door at this time of night, for goodness' sake."

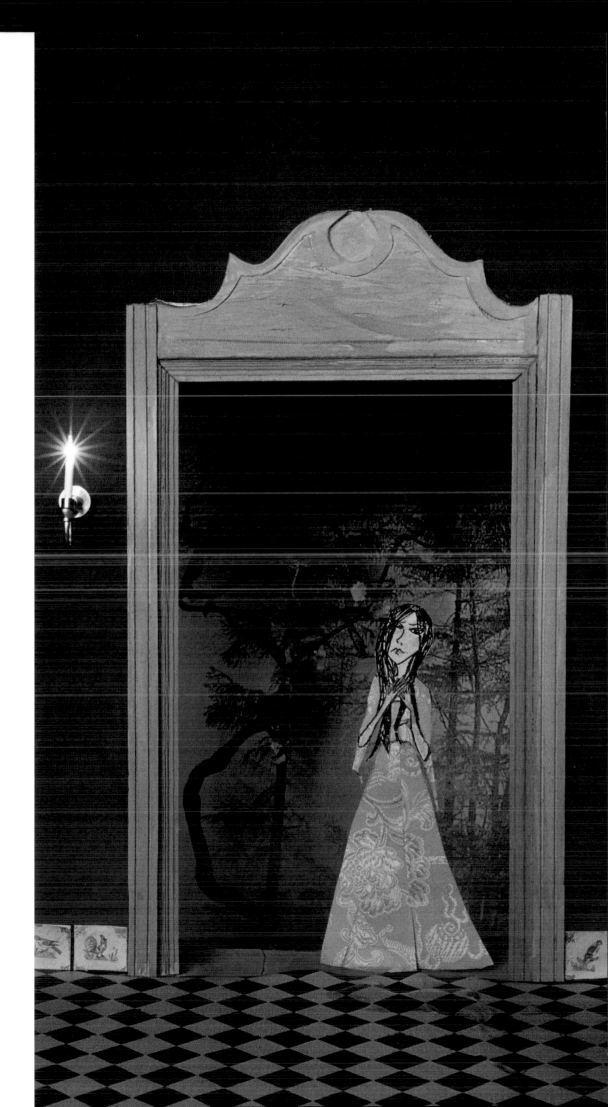

WHEN the king opened the door, what he saw was a dripping-wet girl standing *(without even a coat)* on his doorstep. She had long raven-**black** hair and skin as **pale** as ivory and lips as **red** as rose petals. *You know how it is with these fairy-tale types.* She was, despite the effects of the weather, a *real* beauty. But she was also shivering cold and looked as if she might collapse at any moment.

Of course, the king was very polite. *He had* **manners**. *That's the thing about real kings, their* **manners** *are impeccable.* He didn't even mention the large puddle that was forming on his very expensive royal floor.

*I*NSTEAD
he told the girl
to warm herself
by the fire
while he called
for his wife.

*Who didn't
particularly
want to get up
on such an
unreasonable
night, but being
a real queen
never ever
forgot to be
hospitable
to strangers.*

THE QUEEN THOUGHT this girl looked special, there was something *mesmerizing*, something *fascinating*, something . . . *something* that the queen could not quite put her finger on.

Unlike her husband she came straight to the point. "So, my dear, who are you on such a wild and unruly night?"

"Oh, I am a princess and I live in a tree house on the other side of the mountain."

"A *tree house?*" pondered the king.

"A *princess?*" inquired the queen. "What kind of princess?"

"Oh, I—" replied the girl, "I am a *real* princess. I was outside admiring the *moon* when it started to *rain* and then, what with the *thunder* and *lightning*, well, then I lost my way and then I saw a light in your window . . . I do hope you can forgive my waking you at such an hour."

The queen thought, Well, she **sounds** like a *real* princess, she **looks** like a *real* princess, but we'll see.

So after the girl had finished her elderflower cordial, the queen ordered a steaming-hot bath and supplied her with the softest towels and an exquisite nightgown.

"Oh, this is far too good for me," said the girl, *which, of course, is exactly the kind of thing a* *real* princess *would say.*

WHILE the girl was taking her bath, the queen had the servants make up the bed—in a most unusual fashion.

❧

She chose the most fabulous bedchamber with the most *beautiful* four-poster bed. Then right in the middle of the bed she placed a tiny, tiny pea-green *pea* from the royal garden, then on top of the *pea* she piled one, two, three, four, five, six, seven, eight, nine, ten, eleven, twelve feather mattresses. And on top of the twelve mattresses she placed the *finest* linen sheets and the plumpest Siberian goose-down pillows.

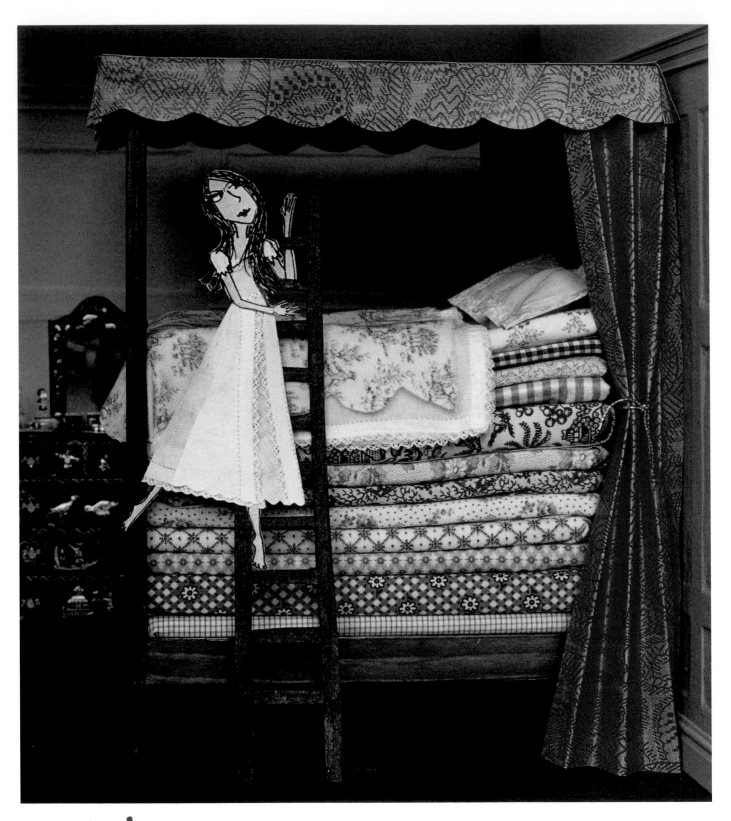

"**W**HAT a beautiful bed," gasped the girl. "Oh, I am sure I will sleep like a *real* **princess** in this bed." And up the ladder she climbed.

We'll see, thought the queen.

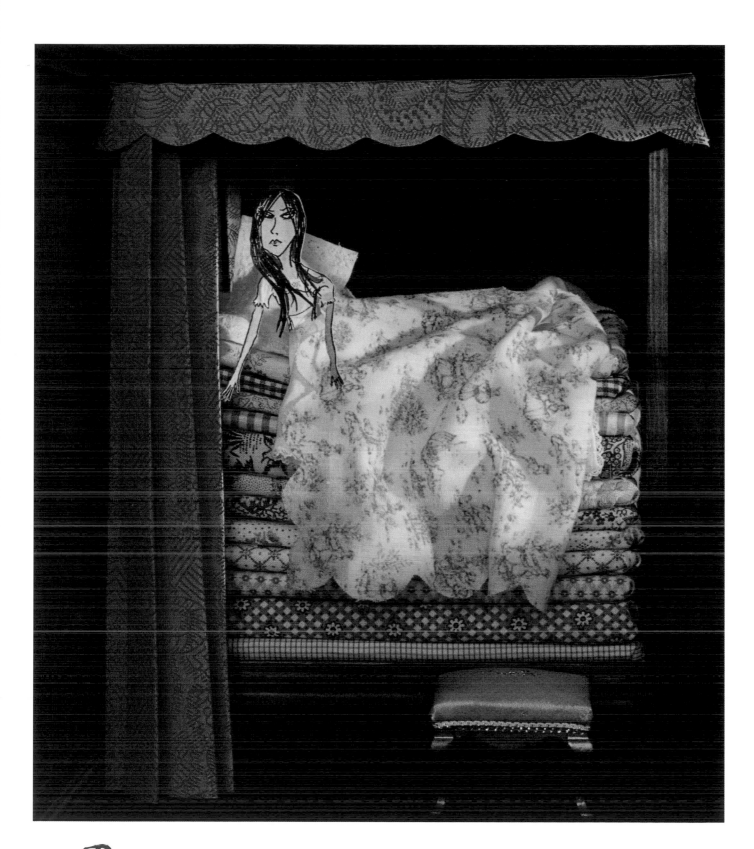

$\mathcal{B}$ UT that night the poor girl hardly slept a wink. She was tossing and turning all night. Despite her exhaustion she could not make herself comfortable. Worse still, the next morning she found she was black and blue and rather achy.

T DAYBREAK THE QUEEN knocked on the door with a cup of tea. "How did you sleep, my dear? I trust comfortably."

Not wanting to be rude, the girl replied, "Oh, very well. Yes, perfectly. Thank you so much for asking."

Aha, thought the queen, I knew she couldn't really be a *real, real* **princess**.

⁂

But what the queen was forgetting was that any real princess has such impeccable manners that it would be impossible for her to tell her host, who had gone to all the effort of making her a bed stacked with twelve feather mattresses, that, in fact, it was the most uncomfortable night that she had ever had, in all her life.

⁂

The queen, though most disappointed, invited her young guest to have breakfast down in the royal dining room.

WHEN the prince saw the girl his eyes lit up.

❧

He thought she was **more** *mesmerizing* **than the** *moon* and when she spoke he found her **more** *fascinating* **than the** *stars.*

❧

And there was a *certain...* *something* about her that caused him to let go of his teacup, which clattered to the floor.

THE PRINCESS COULDN'T help thinking there was

something *romantic,*

something *dramatic,*

something . . . *strangely charming*

about his clumsiness, and she bent down to pick up the cup. A *real* **princess** *will always pick up your teacup if you drop it—kindness is practically their middle name—but this was not the only reason she did so.*

There was a light in the prince's dark eyes that reminded her of

all the *stars* in the night sky.

It did not escape the queen's notice that as the girl bent down she let out a cry something a bit like *ouch.*

"Whatever is the matter, my dear?" asked the king.

"Oh dear, I am all aches and pains today and I just don't know why and I feel so awful when you went to so much effort and how ungrateful I must seem and I hope you will forgive me."

But there was nothing to forgive because, as anyone will know, a girl who

can turn **black** and **blue** when a tiny, tiny **pea-green** garden *pea* is placed

under **twelve** feather mattresses, must just surely be a *real* **princess**.

The prince, who was not very bothered about this detail, simply said,

"There's a *certain something* about you."

❧

And the girl smiled and told him her name.

AND after the
moon had risen
and set several more
times, the prince
asked the girl to
marry him.
That's the thing about
real princes,
they know all the right
questions to ask.

❧

And she being a
bright girl—*as all*
real princesses
are—knew a
real prince
when she saw one,
and said *yes*.

❧

And they were
married in a very
real fashion,
outside in a garden
where the sky
twinkled with *stars*
and the *moon*
shone down and
everyone had
a splendid time.

*P*EAS
were not served because,
as everyone knows,
real princesses
are not especially fond of
peas.

Lauren Child is one of today's most talented and innovative children's writers and illustrators. Winner of the Smarties Prize and the Kate Greenaway Medal, Lauren is best known for her *Clarice Bean* and Charlie and Lola books. Charlie and Lola are now featured in the wonderful animated television series.

Polly Borland is an internationally acclaimed portrait photographer, whose commissions include the Queen, Germaine Greer, and Nick Cave. She has won the John Kobal Portrait Award and is a fellow of the Royal Photographic Society. She has exhibited at the National Portrait Gallery in London as well as in her native Australia.

In this book Lauren has collaborated with Polly to set *The Princess and the Pea* in a miniature, three-dimensional world. The joy for Lauren of working with a photographer like Polly was the ability to capture a moment—so you can almost imagine the characters have just walked into the room.

"I love the paintings of Vermeer, his detail and the way he allows you a glimpse into someone else's world." —LAUREN

"Lauren had a very clear idea of how she wanted each scene to look. As the photographer, my job was to breathe life into them." —POLLY